Dear Parents:

Congratulations! Your child is taking the first steps on an exciting journey. The destination? Independent reading!

STEP INTO READING® will help your child get there. The program offers five steps to reading success. Each step includes fun stories and colorful art or photographs. In addition to original fiction and books with favorite characters, there are Step into Reading Non-Fiction Readers, Phonics Readers and Boxed Sets, Sticker Readers, and Comic Readers—a complete literacy program with something to interest every child.

Learning to Read, Step by Step!

Ready to Read   Preschool–Kindergarten
• big type and easy words • rhyme and rhythm • picture clues
For children who know the alphabet and are eager to begin reading.

Reading with Help   Preschool–Grade 1
• basic vocabulary • short sentences • simple stories
For children who recognize familiar words and sound out new words with help.

Reading on Your Own   Grades 1–3
• engaging characters • easy-to-follow plots • popular topics
For children who are ready to read on their own.

Reading Paragraphs   Grades 2–3
• challenging vocabulary • short paragraphs • exciting stories
For newly independent readers who read simple sentences with confidence.

Ready for Chapters   Grades 2–4
• chapters • longer paragraphs • full-color art
For children who want to take the plunge into chapter books but still like colorful pictures.

STEP INTO READING® is designed to give every child a successful reading experience. The grade levels are only guides; children will progress through the steps at their own speed, developing confidence in their reading.

Remember, a lifetime love of reading starts with a single step!

Visit us on the Web!
StepIntoReading.com
randomhouse.com/kids

Educators and librarians, for a variety of teaching tools, visit us at RHTeachersLibrarians.com

ISBN 978-0-553-50893-2 (trade) — ISBN 978-0-553-50894-9 (lib. bdg.)
ISBN 978-0-553-50895-6 (ebook)

Printed in the United States of America   10 9 8 7 6 5 4 3 2 1

JULIUS Jr.

CrAyon CrAzE!

By Mary Tillworth

Illustrated by Jennifer Song

Random House 🏠 New York

Julius makes a new toy!
He shows it
to Clancy and Worry Bear.

Ping has crayons.
She wants to color.
But her friends want
to play
with the new toy.

Worry Bear gives Ping
his green monkey.
He asks her
to keep it safe.

Ping goes inside.

She opens her crayon box.

Book

She picks
the pink crayon!
Its name is Rosie.

Ping shows Rosie
her pictures.
Ping uses many colors.
Her favorite color
is pink!

Ping and Rosie see a car.

They color the car pink!

Ping and Rosie see
Sheree's oven mitts.

They color

the oven mitts pink!

Ping sees Worry Bear's green monkey.

She has an idea.

After they play,
Ping's friends come inside.
They look around.

The car is pink.

Sheree's mitts are pink.

Worry Bear's monkey
is pink!

Ping gasps.
Her pictures are pink,
too!

Ping and Rosie are sorry
that they colored everything.
Next time,
they will ask first.

How will they solve
the pink problem?
Julius has an idea.

Julius makes a tool
with his new toy
and Ping's crayons.

The new tool
has many colors.
It colors the car.

It colors Sheree's mitts.

Ping colors
Worry Bear's monkey.
The monkey is
green again!

Worry Bear tells Ping
he likes a little pink.
Ping colors a heart.
She colors a headband.
Pink perfect!